Sphinx Pose

Dolphin Pose

Runner's Lunge

Rabbit Pose

Bridge Pose

Crab Pose

Shoulder Stand

Ball Pose

Dragon Pose

Arrow Lunge

Triangle Pose

Bear Pose

Star Pose

Skater Pose

Hero Pose

meditation Pose

ISBN 978-0-06-301784-9

The artist used Adobe Photoshop and Procreate to create
the digital illustrations for this book.
21 22 23 24 25 RTLO 10 9 8 7 6 5 4 3 2 1

First Edition

A special thanks to all of my and Yoga Bunny's friends:
Lisa, Luana, Jeanne, Chrisila, Rick,
and the rest of the team at Harper.
Also, to agent extraordinaire Clelia Gore.

for my
Mama Bear

A Friend for YOGA BUNNY

by Brian Russo

HARPER
An Imprint of HarperCollinsPublishers

Bunny started every morning the same way, doing yoga.
Sometimes he couldn't wait to practice yoga with his
friends. . . .

But some days, like today, Bunny was happy to do yoga all by himself.

He took a deep breath in,

lifted his leg up, up, up,

and gently kicked into
leaf pose.

As he breathed out and opened
his eyes, he saw a great big . . .

BEAR!

"Hello!" said Bunny. "Why are you hiding behind that tree?"
"You see, tomorrow is . . . my birthday," replied Bear shakily.

"Happy birthday!" said Bunny. "Birthdays are great!"
"Not this birthday." Bear sighed.

"My family's throwing me a big party, and I don't like being the center of attention. It makes my paws get sweaty and my heart beat really fast!"

"Well," said Bunny, "whenever you're feeling
anxious or nervous, yoga can help you feel better.
Want to practice with me?"

Bear had never done yoga before, but
she figured it was worth a try.

Bunny showed Bear how to arch her belly to the ground like a cow . . .

how to round her back like a cat . . .

and how to take deeeep breaths in and out.

As they gently flowed from pose to pose, Bear had an idea. "We should make cat and cow noises while doing the poses," she said excitedly. "Or is yoga supposed to be serious?"

Bunny looked up
and let out a big
"MOOOOO!"
Bear smiled.

Then they both rounded
their backs and went,
"MEEEEOW!"

The friends laughed and laughed.

Next, Bunny showed Bear how to do **camel pose.**

They knelt up tall, arched their backs, and pressed their hearts forward to a rainbow in the sky.

Bunny and Bear sat under a tree,
where everything was calm and still.

"It's okay to feel nervous, Bear," said Bunny.
"When my paws get sweaty and my heart beats really
fast . . .

"I just let nervous thoughts or feelings come and go as if they were clouds in the sky."

"Does that work?" asked Bear. "Sometimes," Bunny calmly replied. "I'm doing yoga tomorrow with my friends. You should come!"

Bear wasn't sure about doing yoga with a bunch of animals she didn't know. But she told Bunny she'd think about it.

The next morning, Bunny crawled out of his hole, excited to do yoga. He was especially excited that his new friend might be there.

But Bear wasn't there.

Still, Bunny and his friends closed their eyes, pressed their hands together, and sat quietly through a **meditation warm-up**.

Bunny couldn't stop wondering if he had done something to upset Bear. Then he remembered that it's important to let feelings come during yoga, but it's also important to let them go.

"OMMMM."

Bunny calmed his mind as he breathed in and out.

And when Bunny opened his eyes again,

he saw his new friend sitting right there.

"Bear! I'm so glad you're here," said Bunny.
"I started to practice on my own," said Bear,

"but I realized that yoga, just like my birthday, is better with friends."

And with that, Bear breathed in . . .

and breathed out.

Lion Pose

Cat Pose

Cow Pose

Bird Dog Pose

Bow Pose

Tiger Pose

Fish Pose

Bridge Pose

Side Plank

Three Legged Dog

Warrior Three

Crescent Moon

Ladybug Pose

Goddess Pose

Pelican Pose

Horse Pose